MR MAJEIKA
MUSIC TEACHER

Humphrey Carpenter (1946–2005), the author and creator of *Mr Majeika*, was born and educated in Oxford. He went to a school called the Dragon School where exciting things often happened and there were some very odd teachers – you could even call it magical! He became a full-time writer in 1975 and was the author of many award-winning biographies. As well as the *Mr Majeika* titles, his children's books also included *Shakespeare Without the Boring Bits* and *More Shakespeare Without the Boring Bits*. He wrote plays for radio and theatre and founded the children's drama group The Mushy Pea Theatre Company. He played the tuba, double bass, bass saxophone and keyboard.

Humphrey once said, "The nice thing about being a writer is that you can make magic happen without learning tricks. Words are the only tricks you need. I can write: 'He floated up to the ceiling, and a baby rabbit came out of his pocket, grew wings, and flew away.' And you will believe that it really happened! That's magic, isn't it?"

Books by Humphrey Carpenter

MR MAJEIKA

MR MAJEIKA AND THE DINNER LADY

MR MAJEIKA AND THE GHOST TRAIN

MR MAJEIKA AND THE HAUNTED HOTEL

MR MAJEIKA AND THE LOST SPELL BOOK

MR MAJEIKA AND THE MUSIC TEACHER

MR MAJEIKA AND THE SCHOOL BOOK WEEK

MR MAJEIKA AND THE SCHOOL CARETAKER

MR MAJEIKA AND THE SCHOOL INSPECTOR

MR MAJEIKA AND THE SCHOOL PLAY

MR MAJEIKA AND THE SCHOOL TRIP

MR MAJEIKA JOINS THE CIRCUS

MR MAJEIKA ON THE INTERNET

MR MAJEIKA VANISHES

THE PUFFIN BOOK OF CLASSIC
CHILDREN'S STORIES (Ed.)

SHAKESPEARE WITHOUT THE BORING BITS
MORE SHAKESPEARE WITHOUT THE
BORING BITS

HUMPHREY CARPENTER

Mr Majeika and the Music Teacher

Illustrated by Frank Rodgers

PUFFIN

With thanks to Mrs Bennetts and the school orchestra,
and Mrs Jenks and her class, at St Philip and St James
School, Oxford, for their help with the story. And in
memory of Lucy Tsancheva (1972–1984), who helped so
much with the first Mr Majeika

PUFFIN BOOKS

Published by the Penguin Group
Penguin Books Ltd, 80 Strand, London WC2R 0RL, England
Penguin Group (USA) Inc., 375 Hudson Street, New York, New York 10014, USA
Penguin Group (Canada), 90 Eglinton Avenue East, Suite 700, Toronto, Ontario, Canada M4P 2Y3
(a division of Pearson Penguin Canada Inc.)
Penguin Ireland, 25 St Stephen's Green, Dublin 2, Ireland (a division of Penguin Books Ltd)
Penguin Group (Australia), 250 Camberwell Road, Camberwell, Victoria 3124, Australia
(a division of Pearson Australia Group Pty Ltd)
Penguin Books India Pvt Ltd, 11 Community Centre, Panchsheel Park, New Delhi – 110 017, India
Penguin Group (NZ), 67 Apollo Drive, Rosedale, North Shore 0632, New Zealand
(a division of Pearson New Zealand Ltd)
Penguin Books (South Africa) (Pty) Ltd, 24 Sturdee Avenue, Rosebank, Johannesburg 2196, South Africa

Penguin Books Ltd, Registered Offices: 80 Strand, London WC2R 0RL, England

puffinbooks.com

First published by Viking Kestrel Books 1986
Published in Puffin Books 1987
This edition published 2010 for The Book People Ltd,
Hall Wood Avenue, Haydock, St Helens, WA11 9UL
001 – 10 9 8 7 6 5 4 3 2 1

Text copyright © Humphrey Carpenter, 1986
Illustrations copyright © Frank Rodgers, 1986
All rights reserved

The moral right of the author and illustrator has been asserted

Set in Palatino

Printed in Great Britain by Clays Ltd, St Ives plc

British Library Cataloguing in Publication Data
A CIP catalogue record for this book is available from the British Library

ISBN: 978-0-141-33682-4

www.greenpenguin.co.uk

Mixed Sources
Product group from well-managed
forests and other controlled sources
www.fsc.org Cert no. SA-COC-1592
© 1996 Forest Stewardship Council
FSC

Penguin Books is committed to a sustainable future
for our business, our readers and our planet.
The book in your hands is made from paper
certified by the Forest Stewardship Council.

Contents

1. *Hamish goes shopping*

Hamish Bigmore's parents sat having breakfast, and looking at a letter.

'Pass the butter!' shouted Hamish, who was just as rude at home as he was at school. 'I said, *pass the butter!*'

'Ooh, sorry, dear,' said Hamish's mother. She always gave Hamish everything he wanted, and never complained at his rudeness. Of course this made him worse than ever.

'WILL YOU PASS THE BUTTER!!!' Hamish yelled, because his father was still reading the letter, and hadn't handed the butter dish down the table.

'Terribly sorry, old chap,' said Mr Bigmore, giving his son the butter. 'I was busy reading this. Here, have a look.' He handed his son the letter.

Hamish looked at it. This is what it said.

Dear Parents,

I am sure you will be pleased to know that
next term I shall be joining the staff of St Barty's
School as music teacher. I am going to form a
school orchestra, and I want everyone to play
an instrument in it. Please make sure that your

son or daughter brings an instrument to school
with them.

Yours sincerely

Wilhelmina Worlock

Hamish yawned. 'What a boring letter,'
he said. 'Pass the toast. I said, PASS THE
TOAST!!!' His mother hastily gave it to
him.

'Why is it boring, old chap?' asked Mr
Bigmore. 'I'd have thought you would want
to play an instrument. You always like making
a lot of noise.'

'NO I DON'T!' shouted Hamish at the
top of his voice. 'And anyway,' he went on,
stuffing his mouth full of toast while he spoke,
'plgghhng thrr rrccrrddrr zzz zzhllly.'

'I'm sorry, dear,' said his mother timidly,
'but we can't quite understand what you're
saying. Perhaps if you swallowed that toast
before speaking . . . ?'

Hamish glared and spat out toast. 'What I said was, playing the recorder is silly. You know, "Twinkle, Twinkle, Little Star", "Baa, Baa, Black Sheep" — that's all just rubbish for babies.' He crammed some more toast into his mouth.

'I suppose so, old chap,' said his father. 'Could you pass me the milk jug, old fellow, if you please?'

'No,' grunted Hamish. 'I'm busy eating.'

Hamish's father got up and fetched the milk jug for himself. 'But you know,' he said, 'they may play grown-up tunes in the orchestra. This Miss Worlock doesn't say anything about "Twinkle, Twinkle, Little Star". And she doesn't mention recorders. As far as I can see, she'll let you play anything you like.'

Hamish thought for a moment. 'Well, what else *is* there?' he asked.

'I suppose you could play the violin,' said his father.

'Violins are *silly*,' sneered Hamish.

'Or a clarinet,' said his mother.

'That's just a silly sort of recorder with knobs stuck on it,' said Hamish. 'You can't fool me.'

'A flute makes a very pretty noise,' said his father.

'Pretty!' sneered Hamish. 'I don't want to play anything pretty.'

'No, I'm sure not, dear,' said his mother hastily. 'But don't worry. I'm sure we can find something for you. After all, think of all the instruments there are in orchestras – trumpets, oboes, cellos, horns, harps, double basses –'

'Double basses?' said Hamish. 'What are they?'

'Oh, very big things,' said his father. 'Far

too big for someone your age. They're very tall, like huge violins, and they make a deep noise when you pluck them or play them with a bow. But if I were you I'd choose a —'

'I WANT A DOUBLE BASS!!!' shouted Hamish Bigmore.

*

'Music teacher?' said Mr Potter, the headmaster of St Barty's Primary School. 'What music teacher? I don't know anything about any music teacher.'

It was the first day of term, and Mr Potter's office had filled up with angry parents.

'I just can't afford to get expensive musical instruments for my children,' grumbled the mother of Melanie, one of the children in Class Three. 'It costs too much. Who does she think she is, this new music teacher?'

'Yes,' said the other mums and dads crossly, 'you never told us about her.'

'And no one told *me*,' said Mr Potter. '*I*
don't know anything about a new music
teacher. Here, let me see the letter.'

Someone passed him the letter from Miss
Wilhelmina Worlock. 'What a very curious
name,' said Mr Potter, looking at it. 'I didn't

ask her to come to St Barty's. I wonder who did?'

*

There was a dreadful amount of noise going on in Class Three. Squeaks, grunts, groans, rattles, thumps and whistles. Everyone was playing their musical instruments.

'Do be quiet,' called out Thomas to everyone else. 'I can see Mr Majeika coming down the passage.'

'If he hears all this racket,' said Pete, who was Thomas's twin, 'I'm sure he'll turn us all into frogs or snakes or something. You know what he can do when he's *really* cross.'

Mr Majeika was the Class Three teacher, and he had once been a wizard, though he didn't want anyone to know this. Last term he had lost his temper twice with Hamish Bigmore. The first time he had turned a ruler that Hamish was holding into a snake. The

second time he had turned Hamish himself
into a frog. Mr Majeika didn't mean to do
things like that; he said he'd given up magic,
and was trying to be an ordinary teacher. But
sometimes he forgot himself, and things
happened.

'Good morning, everyone,' said Mr
Majeika, coming into the classroom. 'I hope
you all had a good holiday. But what was all

that noise, and why have you all got musical instruments?'

'It's the new music teacher,' said Jody. 'She wrote to our mums and dads.'

'But Mr Potter doesn't know anything about it,' said Thomas.

'And my mum won't buy an instrument for me,' said Melanie, who was always crying. 'Boo-hoo!' She burst into tears as usual.

'It all sounds a bit peculiar,' said Mr Majeika. 'But I suppose it will be good for you all to learn some music.'

'I've got a penny whistle,' said Jody, playing a few notes on it.

Other voices spoke up round the class:

'I've got a trumpet my mum brought from a junk shop, but I can't play it yet.'

'I've got a violin, and my dad says he'll teach me.'

'I've got my sister's old guitar.'

16

'All right,' said Mr Majeika. 'That'll do for now. Put everything away, until this music teacher arrives. And now get your workbooks out and –'

He was interrupted by an odd sort of bumping noise at the door of the classroom. He went over and opened the door.

The doorway was blocked by something very big, made of wood.

'What on earth is this?' said Mr Majeika.

A voice spoke from behind the big wooden thing: 'It's my double bass.' It was Hamish Bigmore.

'Good gracious!' said Mr Majeika. 'Well, you'd better not bring it in here.'

But already Hamish had staggered into the classroom, clutching the enormous musical instrument.

Behind him marched his proud mother and father. 'We always want him to have the best of everything,' said Hamish's father.

'And he *asked* for a double bass,' said Hamish's mother. 'So of course we *had* to get him one.'

Hamish dropped the double bass carelessly on to the floor, and then fell over it.

'Careful, old man,' said his father. 'It cost a lot of money, you know.'

'Shut up, silly!' said Hamish Bigmore. 'It's *my* double bass, and I can do what I like with it.'

'Hamish Bigmore,' said Mr Majeika, 'don't speak to your parents in that fashion. Leave that thing where it is, and sit down in your place. Mr and Mrs Bigmore, I would be obliged if you could remove this musical instrument from the classroom. I can't imagine that the music teacher, whoever she is, will want to have such an object in her orchestra. Apart from anything else, your son isn't big enough to play it.'

'Rubbish!' shouted Hamish Bigmore. 'Of course I am. And of course Miss Worlock will want me to play it. You see if she doesn't.'

Thomas and Pete felt certain that Mr

19

Majeika would lose his temper. In fact he had turned quite white. But he didn't seem angry at all. Instead, he seemed to be frightened.

'Miss — what did you say?' he asked Hamish in an odd sort of voice.

'Miss Worlock,' said Hamish. 'The new music teacher. Miss Wilhelmina Worlock.'

'Wilhelmina Worlock?' said Mr Majeika, putting his hand on his head as if he had a headache. 'Oh, *no!*'

'What's the matter?' asked Pete. 'Have you heard of her?'

'Heard of her?' answered Mr Majeika. 'Oh yes, I've heard of her. I've heard of her all right. Wilhelmina Worlock is a witch.'

2. *The letter on the mat*

It was Jody who found the letter. She was passing the main door of the school at break time, and she saw it lying on the mat, as if it had just come through the letter-box. It was addressed in spidery handwriting:

To Mr Potter

Head Teacher

St Barty's School

URGENT

Anyone who delays this letter from arriving FAST will be turned into a TOAD.

Jody thought this last bit was very odd, but she supposed she had better take it to Mr Potter's office at once.

She knocked on the door. 'What is it?' grumbled Mr Potter. He had forgotten all about the mysterious matter of the music teacher, and was trying to add up the term's dinner and swimming money, and wondering why it came out differently every time.

'A letter for you, Mr Potter,' said Jody, handing him the envelope. 'It looks a bit funny to me.'

'Funny?' said Mr Potter crossly. 'What's funny about a letter? I don't see anything funny at all.' He ripped the envelope open crossly.

What happened next was very strange indeed. Something that looked like a photograph fell out of the envelope on to Mr Potter's desk. It was a picture of an old woman with long, straggly, grey hair and gold-rimmed glasses. Jody thought how ugly she looked. Then suddenly the picture began to grow – not just to get bigger, but to become

fatter, so that it was no longer a picture at all
but a real person. In a moment, the old woman
herself was standing in Mr Potter's office.

'Good gracious,' said Mr Potter, scratching
his head. 'Where did you come from, madam?'

'In the post, dearie,' said the old lady
cheerfully. 'A nice cheap way to travel, for
those of us who can manage it. You get a

comfy night's rest in an envelope, and then, hey presto, there you are at your destination! And it only costs a first-class stamp. *Much* less fuss than a broomstick. But I forgot – my card.'

She held her hand up in the air, and in it, from nowhere, there suddenly appeared a small white card. She handed it to Mr Potter. 'There you are, dearie,' she said.

Mr Potter looked at it. It read:

WILHELMINA W. WORLOCK

DipW, LRCW

Music Teaching For All Ages

on the So-Spooky Method

Terms: Cash Weekly

Mr Potter scratched his head. 'Would you be the lady who sent out letters to the parents?' he asked.

'That's right, dearie,' said Miss Worlock.

'Ah,' said Mr Potter thoughtfully.

He turned to Jody. 'I need to have a word with Miss — Miss Worlock in private,' he said.

'Yes, Mr Potter,' answered Jody, and ran off to tell Class Three the extraordinary thing she had seen.

'Now,' said Mr Potter, closing the door of his office, 'I'm afraid there is some misunderstanding, my good lady. I didn't arrange for you to come and teach music, and I shan't be able to take you on to the staff. I'm sorry you've been troubled. Good day to you.'

He held out his hand. But Miss Worlock didn't shake it. She just giggled: 'Tee-hee!'

'Ugh!' cried Mr Potter, springing back. In his hand was a live toad.

He put it hastily on to his desk and wiped his hand on his trousers. Miss Worlock picked it up and stroked it. 'Come to Mother,' she said cooingly. 'Didn't nasty man like you?'

'As I was saying,' said Mr Potter, breathing heavily, 'we don't require you here. Would you please take yourself off the school premises?' He opened the office door to show her out.

'Tee-hee!' said Miss Worlock.

'Ow!' said Mr Potter, because his hand had begun to sting. He tried to take it off the door-handle. It wouldn't come. It was stuck fast.

'Did you say you wanted me to go? And that you didn't want me to teach music, eh?' said Miss Worlock, pushing her beady eyes unpleasantly near Mr Potter's face. He tried to back away but couldn't, being still stuck to the door.

'That's right,' said Mr Potter uncomfortably. 'We have no need of you here. So kindly be on your way right now.' With his free hand, he pointed at the open doorway — and then cried out, 'Ugh!' again.

On the end of his finger was a large black
spider.

'Take it off!' yelled Mr Potter, who, even
though he was a headmaster, was terrified of
spiders.

'Tee-hee!' said Miss Worlock. 'It can stay

there, and you can stay stuck there, till you decide that Wilhelmina Worlock is just the person you need to teach music at St Barty's school.'

*

'And she came out of the envelope,' said Jody breathlessly, 'and grew and *grew*, and there she was just standing there, and she looks horrid, just like a witch!'

Mr Majeika nodded gloomily. 'That sounds exactly like Wilhelmina Worlock,' he said.

'Do you know her well?' asked Thomas.

'All too well,' said Mr Majeika miserably. 'A particularly nasty type of witch. In fact a horrid old crone, not to put too fine a point on it.'

'But you were a wizard,' said Thomas, 'and *you* didn't do horrid things, did you?'

Mr Majeika shook his head. 'I was a white magician,' he explained. 'Wilhelmina Worlock does black magic — or at least fairly dirty grey. I wouldn't want to set eyes on her again.' He shuddered.

'Well,' said Pete, 'I expect Mr Potter will soon get rid of her.'

'I wonder,' said Mr Majeika.

*

Mr Potter was still trapped in his office with Miss Worlock. He had agreed that she could teach music at St Barty's, in return for which she set him free from the door-handle and took the spider off his finger. 'Pretty little thing,' she cooed at it, tucking it into her pocket. 'Now,' she said briskly to Mr Potter, 'I want you to pay me a hundred pounds a week.'

'Ridiculous!' spluttered Mr Potter. 'Thirty pounds for two mornings' work is all I can possibly manage.' He took out his handkerchief to mop his head — and found to his horror that it was full of big slimy worms.

'Uggh!' he cried, shaking them on to the carpet.

Miss Worlock gathered them lovingly, and put them in her pocket along with the toad and the spider. 'Aren't they sweet?' she purred.

'Well, fifty pounds,' said Mr Potter, and sat down wearily in his chair – leaping to his feet

almost at once, because a live crab, appearing from nowhere, had attached its claws to his bottom. 'Ow!' he cried. 'I've had enough of this! Take a hundred pounds a week, then, you wretched woman, though goodness knows how I can pay you. But get out of my office!'

'Tee-hee!' said Miss Worlock. 'Don't worry,

dearie, I'm off! But you never asked about the letters on my card.'

'Letters?' said Mr Potter weakly.

'DipW,' said Miss Worlock, 'and LRCW. My qualifications. They stand for "Diploma in Witchcraft" and "Licensed by the Royal College of Witches". But I expect you could have guessed that by now. Tee-hee! Bye-bye!'

3. The orchestra

'What I don't understand,' said Jody gloomily, 'is why a witch should want to come to St Barty's.'

'Mr Majeika thinks it's probably for the same reason that *he* came,' said Thomas. 'He says you can't make any money as a magician these days. You've got to get some other job. But it's an awful pity that she chose St Barty's.'

They were walking across the playground to the school hall for the first rehearsal of Miss Worlock's orchestra.

'Here,' shouted a voice, 'give me a hand with my double bass.' It was Hamish Bigmore.

Thomas and Pete, who only had recorders to carry, unwillingly picked up the big instrument. 'Quick march!' snapped Hamish. 'Get on with it.'

'*You're* only carrying the little end,'
grumbled Pete.

In the hall, Miss Worlock was putting music
on the music-stands. 'Ugh,' muttered Thomas,
'I think she looks *horrid*.'

'Not at all,' said Hamish. 'I think she looks
very nice indeed. Not like silly old Mr
Majeika.'

One by one, the other children arrived.
'Quiet, everyone!' called Miss Worlock when
they were all there. 'I am your new music

teacher.' She smiled a horrible smile. 'You may like to know a little about my method. There are all kinds of ways of teaching music. There's the Sol-Fa method. That means you learn the names of the notes: Doh, Ray, Me, Fa, Sol. That's all rubbish, and I don't want to waste time with it. There's also the Suzuki method. That was invented by a Japanese person, and we're not in Japan, so we don't want to know about that. *My* method is called the So-Spooky method. Can anyone guess what *that* means?'

There was silence. Only Class Three knew that Miss Worlock was a witch, but everyone could see she was a thoroughly nasty person.

'The So-Spooky method,' went on Miss Worlock, 'means that you've got to practise your instruments very hard, otherwise something oh-so-spooky will happen to you.

Have you got that clear? Very well, let's get on with the music.'

Everyone picked up their instruments.

'This term,' said Miss Worlock, 'we're going to learn a piece of music called "The Carnival of the Animals". We'll begin straight away. And I want you to play the right notes, or else ...'

She sat down at the piano. 'The first piece is a March,' she called out. 'Off we go. One, two, three, four.'

She began to play.

A terrible noise rose up all round the hall. Recorders squeaked like mice caught in a trap, violins scraped like rusty door-hinges, clarinets howled like dogs calling to the moon, trumpets blared like lorries hooting in a traffic jam. 'STOP!' shouted Miss Worlock after a moment. 'That's *terrible*! Didn't you listen to

my warning? Now, play the right notes, or
you'll know what the So-Spooky method
means soon enough. Off we go again. One,
two, three, four.'

This time the noise was even worse. 'Eee-
ooo-uuu-iii-eee!' squeaked the recorders.

'Zzee-zzii-zzyy!' scraped the violins. 'Wwoo-wwuu-wwoo!' howled the clarinets. 'Raa-raa-raaaaaaaa!' blared the trumpets.

'That's ENOUGH!' screamed Miss Worlock. 'Toads! That's what I ought to turn you into! Horrid slimy toads, every one of you! I've never heard such a noise in all my life.'

A hand went up at the back. It was Jody. 'Please, miss,' she said, 'it's not *our* fault. You told us to get instruments, and bring them to school, but you haven't taught us how to play them properly. Most of us have never done music before.'

'That's right,' murmured everyone. 'We just don't know how to play.'

Miss Worlock glared at them. 'Well then, teach yourselves!' she snarled. 'You're not babies. Take the instruments home, and *find out* how to play them. If you can't discover by yourselves, then get a *book*. You idiots! Any questions?'

'Yes, miss.' It was a rather cheeky girl from Mr Majeika's class called Clare. 'You're the music teacher, so you're supposed to teach us, aren't you?'

'Do you want to be turned into something very nasty?' sneered Miss Worlock at her. 'No? Then don't be rude. Any more complaints?'

'No complaints at all,' said a voice from the back of the orchestra. It was Hamish Bigmore. 'Anyone can play properly if they try. Look!' And he began to saw away at his double bass, *pom pom, pom pom, pom pom, pom pom*. It was just the same two notes, again and again. He had propped the big instrument up in a corner, and was using two hands on the bow – he wasn't nearly tall enough to reach the top of the strings and change the notes. *Pom pom, pom pom, pom pom, pom pom.*

Everyone began to laugh.

'Silence!' screamed Miss Worlock. 'Well, at least there's one person who takes his music seriously. Well done!' she called out to Hamish Bigmore. 'In fact it looks as if you're going to be my star pupil.'

*

After that, Miss Worlock made the orchestra practise for hours and hours every morning, even though Mr Potter said that music was only supposed to be on Thursdays. But all he got for his trouble was a pocket full of black beetles. Miss Worlock told him she'd think of something nastier if he didn't shut up. He went to his office and locked the door, to hide from the horrible music teacher. He tried to work out how he could find a hundred pounds to give her each week. In the end he decided

41

to sack two of the dinner ladies, and give her their wages. But that meant that he had to serve out dinner himself.

The worst time for the children in the orchestra wasn't, however, the practices with Miss Worlock, but the weekend. Thomas and Pete took their recorders home with them, because Miss Worlock had told the orchestra that everyone must practise hard on Saturday and Sunday. At first they forgot all about it and went off to play football, or on bike rides. However, by lunch time on Saturday, Pete complained to Thomas that his fingers were itching very nastily.

'Mine too,' said Thomas. 'I wonder if it's chickenpox.'

Then, almost by chance, Thomas picked up his recorder, when he was looking for something in the sitting-room, and the itching stopped. He called Pete, and Pete found that *his* itchy fingers stopped when he picked up *his* recorder.

'Oh dear,' said Pete, 'I'm afraid that this is her So-Spooky method. She's going to *make* us practise.'

Sure enough, on Monday morning everyone else complained that they'd itched all weekend, till they'd done at least two hours' practice on their instruments.

Because everyone was working so hard at their music, the orchestra was quite a bit better on Monday, and most of the instruments sounded less like animals screaming. But it was still a fairly terrible noise and Miss Worlock looked as angry as ever.

'"Carnival of the Animals" indeed!' she snarled, after they had tried to play the March yet again. 'The best you'll ever sound like is a herd of elephants.' Then suddenly her eyes lit up. 'Elephants!' she cried. '"The Elephant!"'

And she turned to Hamish Bigmore. 'You alone,' she told him, 'are making a nice noise on your instrument. And *you* shall be the star performer. You shall play the solo in the best of all the tunes in "The Carnival of the Animals", the tune that's called "The Elephant". Listen!'

And Miss Worlock sat down at the piano and played a heavy, lumbering tune that

certainly sounded very like an elephant walking up and down: 'Rum-tum-tum, tum-tiddle-iddle, um-tum-tum-tum ...'

When she had finished, she turned to Hamish and said: 'Do you think you can play that?'

Hamish grinned. 'I'm sure I can,' he said, 'if I have some help. Give me two people to change the notes – they'll do' (and he pointed at Thomas and Pete) 'and I'll play "The Elephant" better than you've ever heard it!'

*

And so, much against their will, Thomas and Pete found themselves Hamish Bigmore's slaves. 'We have to do all the real work,' grumbled Thomas, 'while he just stands there and pulls his bow to and fro.'

They had to stand on chairs, one on each side of the double bass, and, while Hamish sawed to and fro with the bow, they had to

do all the tricky work of putting the right
strings down with their fingers. Naturally
they often made mistakes, and Miss Worlock
shouted and screamed at them, and threatened
to turn them into toads and other nasty things.
Meanwhile she petted Hamish Bigmore, and
told him how marvellous he was.

'What I can't understand,' Pete said to Hamish one morning, after they had been sweating for hours at 'The Elephant', 'is why you're being so nice to her. Can't you see she's a horrid old bag who means no good to anyone?'

'Of course I can,' grinned Hamish. 'But just think what *I'm* going to get out of it. She's told me that if I play well in the concert at the end of term, she'll teach me everything.'

'Teach you everything?' repeated Thomas. 'Do you mean music?'

'No, idiot,' sneered Hamish. 'I mean magic. I'm going to get my revenge on Mr Majeika. By the time I'm finished, I'll have learnt how to turn him into a frog. Just you see!'

4. Trouble in the staffroom

'Please,' said Jody to Mr Majeika, 'you must do something. Otherwise Hamish will learn to be a black magician, and we'll none of us be safe.'

'Oh dear!' Mr Majeika said, scratching his head gloomily.

'Surely you want Miss Worlock out of the school as much as everyone else does?' said Pete.

Mr Majeika nodded. 'She's quite impossible,' he said. 'She's taken over the staffroom, and she keeps cooking horrible spells and things in there. None of us dares go in, the smell is so nasty. And we can't get on with teaching our classes, she's always having orchestra practice all the time.'

'Couldn't you get rid of her by magic?'

asked Jody. 'I mean, you must know some spells that she doesn't. Wouldn't that get rid of her?'

Mr Majeika looked doubtful. 'Spells are tricky things,' he said. 'They often go wrong, or don't work in the way you intend them to. But I suppose I could have a try . . .'

He set off nervously for the staffroom, Thomas, Pete and Jody following him. He seemed very anxious, and was obviously glad to have them with him.

Outside the staffroom, two of the other teachers were hanging about, looking fed up. 'We want to make some coffee,' one of them said, 'but we can't go in because of *her*.'

Nobody needed to ask who was meant by 'her'. Even in the passage, the smell was terrible. And when Mr Majeika opened the door, clouds of steam and green-looking smoke came billowing out.

'Tee-hee,' said a voice from inside, 'come
and have elevenses with Auntie Wilhelmina!'

Anxiously, they all stepped inside. Miss
Worlock had taken over the whole room. She
had lit a fire in the fireplace, and bubbling on
it was a cauldron of foul-smelling stuff, all
green and scummy.

'Have a cup of Auntie's Morning Mixture!' said Miss Worlock, who seemed to be much more friendly when she wasn't teaching music. She dipped a mug into the cauldron and handed it to Mr Majeika.

Thomas could see that there were nasty-looking things swimming about in it. 'What is it?' he asked.

'Oh, just a touch of this and a dash of that, dearie. Tee-hee!' said Miss Worlock, pointing at an assortment of half-opened tins scattered around the table. They were labelled, Eye of Newt, Bats' Tongues in Tomato Sauce, Curried Frog Spawn, and Pigs' Ears in Ditchwater (with added Vitamin C).

'Yuck!' said the children. But Mr Majeika, wanting to be polite, had taken the steaming mug from Miss Worlock.

'One lump or two?' asked Miss Worlock, holding out what looked like a sugar bowl.

'Two, please,' said Mr Majeika – and then he sprang back in horror, as she dropped two evil-looking things into his mug. 'What are those?' he cried.

'Oh, just a little thing I put together myself,' cackled Miss Worlock. 'Black beetles coated with mouldy cheese. I've got a deep freeze full of them at home.'

'I, er, I don't think they would agree with me,' said Mr Majeika unsteadily, putting down his mug. 'Now, er, Wilhelmina, you and I are old acquaintances, I wouldn't exactly say friends, but –'

'Not friends, no, dearie,' Miss Worlock screeched merrily. 'Do you remember the time on Walpurgis Night when I –'

'Don't remind me!' said Mr Majeika, looking pale. 'But what I have come to say is this. St Barty's School already has one wizard, that is, me, and any magic that's to be done here is my concern. There isn't room for two of us. You've no right to come barging in here like this and making such a terrible nuisance of yourself. Now, be a good witch – er, music teacher – and pack your bags and leave us in peace.'

'What a pretty speech!' cackled Miss Worlock. 'And what do you intend to do about it, pray, my fine wizard?'

'Do about it?' asked Mr Majeika anxiously.

'How do you intend to get me out of here, you *white wizard*?' Miss Worlock said these last words so that they sounded the rudest thing in the world.

'Well, that is, er,' muttered Mr Majeika, 'I do have my magic powers.'

'Magic powers? Magic powers?' cackled Miss Worlock. 'You think that *you* can get *me* out of here by magic? Just you try! Tee-hee!' And, with these words, she suddenly flew up into the air and landed on top of the bookcase. 'Go on!' she sneered. 'Show me!'

'Oh dear,' sighed Mr Majeika. 'I was afraid it would come to this. Er, let me think, now. Well, I suppose ...' And, after considering the matter for a moment, he suddenly flung one hand out in front of him.

From his fingers there leapt a blue flame. It crackled and danced about the room, lighting up Miss Worlock's cooking pot and tins, fizzing round the table and the bookshelves, and finally settling on Miss Worlock herself, who seemed about to go up in flames as the blue fire crackled and sizzled over her from top to toe.

But Miss Worlock merely looked bored, and yawned, and after a few moments the blue fire died away. Mr Majeika seemed tired after the effort of making it, but Miss Worlock was quite unharmed.

'Phosphorescent fire?' she laughed horribly. 'Is that all you can do? Lawks, dearie, you can buy that stuff at Tesco's now. I can see I've got a thing or two to teach you.' And she pointed her finger at Mr Majeika, in just the same way that he had jabbed his arm towards her.

Thomas, Pete and Jody expected poor Mr Majeika to burst into flames. But in fact nothing at all happened and he looked as relieved as they did, and put his hand into his pocket to get a handkerchief to wipe his forehead. Then suddenly he cried: 'Ugh! What's *this*?' And the children could see that his hand was covered with a nasty mess.

'Hamish Bigmore's lunch,' cackled Miss Worlock from the top of the bookcase. 'Or at least, what he left on his plate. Half-chewed sausage, mushy peas, and mashed potato. You'll find it all in your pocket, dearie – by magic!'

It was true. Mr Majeika's pocket had suddenly become full of messy food. 'What a horrid trick,' said Jody. 'But can't you think of something else to do to her, Mr Majeika?'

Mr Majeika sighed, then said: 'Well, this might work.' And he began to chant some strange words in a low voice.

Instantly the room became dark, and a cold wind seemed to blow through it. The children thought they could no longer be indoors. They seemed to have been transported to a cold, bleak moorland, with a storm blowing all around them. Then, in the distance, they heard a terrible howling which all too quickly

was getting dreadfully near. In a moment, out
of the mist there loomed red eyes. Huge
shapes could be seen, and Jody cried out:
'Wolves!' The dreadful animals howled and
snarled as they bounded past the children, and
Thomas and Pete expected to see them snatch

up Miss Worlock in their jaws and tear her to bits.

But suddenly the mist cleared, and the children saw that they were all still in the staffroom at St Barty's. Miss Worlock, quite unharmed, was sitting on the bookcase, eating from a packet labelled Best Dog Biscuits, Made from Fresh Dog.

'Feeble stuff,' she laughed at Mr Majeika. 'Wolves in the mist! Why, I've seen that sort of thing done better on "Blue Peter". Having a bit of trouble with your trousers, dearie?'

Mr Majeika looked down anxiously at his trousers. Sure enough, a nasty mess was dripping out of his other pocket. 'Hamish Bigmore's pudding,' said Miss Worlock cheerfully. 'Stewed rhubarb. Any more tricks to amuse me?'

'Oh dear,' sighed Mr Majeika. 'Well, I suppose ...' And again, he muttered something strange under his breath, and once more the room became dark.

This time they were still indoors, but there was the thump of heavy feet, *thump*, *thump*, *thump*, and a voice chanting familiar words:

Fee, fi, fo, fum,
I smell the blood of an Englishwoman.
Be she alive or be she dead —

'Oh, come off it, dearie,' cackled Miss Worlock, and the voice faded and the room became light again. 'Don't give me that old one. Any party conjuror can do *that*. You ventriloquists really have had your day, you know. Why, you should see some of those new computer games. They really can teach us oldies a thing or two! Now, be off with you and don't come interfering with me any more. I'm here to stay, dearie, and you'd better get used to it, tee-hee! By the way, don't you think you ought to change your socks?'

Mr Majeika peered down at his feet. 'Oh dear,' he said. 'There does seem to be something squelchy in them. Not Hamish Bigmore again?'

'That's right, dearie,' answered Miss Worlock. 'The custard from his rhubarb. You'll find it all in your shoes.'

'Ugh!' cried Mr Majeika. 'I've had enough.' And he fled from the staffroom, closely followed by Thomas, Pete and Jody.

'Oh dear,' said Jody, 'there's no stopping her.'

5. The concert

Miss Worlock's orchestra practised every day.
After Mr Majeika had lost his battle with her,
nobody else tried to interfere. Mr Potter kept
well away, hidden in his office, except when
he came out to serve school dinner. No one
else dared to tangle with her, and she was
allowed to get on with the music whenever
she wanted.

She never exactly became good tempered,
but at least she stopped threatening to turn
the children into toads if they didn't play well
enough. And in fact by now the orchestra was
sounding pretty good. Everyone only had to
go 'um-pum-pum, um-pum-pum' on their
instruments while Hamish Bigmore played
the tune of 'The Elephant' on his double bass
(with Thomas and Pete doing all the hard

work at the top end). But at first the 'um-pum-
pum' had sounded pretty terrible, and now it
was pretty good. As a result Miss Worlock
was in a good mood most of the time, and
anyone who had listened in to the orchestra
practice would probably have thought that
she was a perfectly ordinary music teacher.

Towards the end of term she put up a
notice, which said:

CONCERT
by the ST BARTY'S SCHOOL ORCHESTRA
conducted by
WILHELMINA WORLOCK
Demonstration of the So-Spooky Method
Miss Worlock's star pupil
HAMISH BIGMORE
will play 'The Elephant' on his double bass
All Parents Welcome

Thomas and Pete looked very gloomy as
the concert approached. 'I know she'll turn us

into toads if we don't work the strings right on Hamish's stupid double bass,' groaned Thomas.

'That's right,' said Pete. 'The whole thing depends on us. If we do our job properly, he'll play the right notes. But she won't thank us. It's her "star pupil" who'll get the praise. And we know what *that* means.'

'Yes, we know what that means,' said Hamish Bigmore, coming up behind them. 'It means she's going to teach me all her secrets! So if she doesn't turn you into toads during the concert, *I* will afterwards!'

On the evening of the concert, Jody found Mr Majeika walking up and down miserably outside the school hall. 'Isn't there anything you can do?' she asked him sadly.

Mr Majeika shook his head. 'Really, I've tried to think of every trick in the book, but there's nothing that can stop her. It isn't that

she's a cleverer wizard than me. It's just that
she's got such a nasty mind. She thinks of
horrid things I'd never dream of. What can
you do against someone like that?'

'Oh, but Mr Majeika,' said Jody, 'do try
please!'

*

The hall was full of parents waiting for the
concert to begin. They'd all been surprised at
how hard their children had practised and
they wanted to hear the results.

The orchestra took their seats and sat as
quiet as mice. Then in came Miss Worlock,
leading Hamish Bigmore. He was dressed in
a smart suit and a bow tie, just like someone
playing in a real orchestra. He was followed
by his double bass. Or rather, he was followed
by Thomas and Pete, carrying the double bass
for him.

Miss Worlock smiled her horrible smile at
the audience who clapped politely. 'Good
evening, ladies and gentlemen,' she said.
'Welcome to the first concert by the St Barty's
School orchestra, who will demonstrate the

success of my So-Spooky method of music
teaching. May I introduce my star pupil,
Hamish Bigmore, who will play "The
Elephant" from "The Carnival of Animals"?
Hamish has been my star pupil this term, and
after the concert I shall reward him by teaching
him *a lot more*! Tee-hee!' She turned to the

orchestra. 'And if you don't all play the right notes,' she snarled at them, 'you know what will happen to you. Toads, every one of you! And as for you two,' she turned to Thomas and Pete, 'worse than toads for you, if you don't play the right notes. I'll make you into insects. So watch it!'

She sat down at the piano, rapped her knuckles on the lid to call for complete silence, then played the first notes of 'The Elephant'. The whole orchestra joined in with her.

'*Um*-pum-pum, *um*-pum-pum,' went the recorders, the violins, the clarinets and the trumpets. And then the double bass began to play: '*Rum*-tum-tum, *tum*-tiddle-iddle, *rum*-tum-tum ...'

Hamish Bigmore sawed away with his bow. And, up at the top end, Thomas and Pete pressed their fingers on the strings so that he played the right notes.

Everything seemed to be going all too well.

Then Pete, out of the corner of his eye, noticed the door at the back of the hall opening, and Mr Majeika slipping quietly in. A moment later, Mr Majeika had *vanished* — he didn't go out of the door again, but just disappeared, in an instant!

A few moments later, the trouble started.

Hamish Bigmore, sawing away with his double bass bow, stopped playing for a moment, then went on again. Miss Worlock glared at him.

'There was a fly on the end of his nose,' whispered Thomas.

'*Rum*-rum-tum, *tum*-tiddle-iddle ...' And again, Hamish stopped for a moment. This time he slapped the end of his nose. The fly flew off.

Miss Worlock glared at him again. He hastily began to play once more. '*Rum*-tum-tum —' And a third time he stopped playing, now scratching his nose in fury.

The whole orchestra stopped. Miss Worlock was in a towering rage. 'What's going on?' she screeched at Hamish. 'Why aren't you playing properly?'

'There's — there's a fly on my nose!' stammered Hamish.

'A fly?' Miss Worlock shouted. 'Why should a fly stop you? Get on with it, boy, and if I have any more trouble you know what'll happen to you.'

'But — but I'm your star pupil,' spluttered Hamish. 'You can't do anything nasty to me.'

'Oh, *can't* I?' sneered Miss Worlock. 'That's what *you* think. Let me tell you, Hamish Bigmore, I'm not going to teach you any of my secrets after this, and if you don't want to be turned into a you-know-what, you'd better not make any mistakes again. Now, back to the beginning everyone.'

She began to play the piano once more, and Hamish and the orchestra joined in. '*Rum*-tum-tum, *tum*-tiddle-iddle . . .'

This time, Hamish didn't stop. But Thomas and Pete could see that he was still having trouble with the fly. He was puffing and blowing out of the corner of his mouth, in an

attempt to get it off the end of his nose. But
it went on sitting there, walking up and down
and tickling him as if it knew perfectly well
the trouble it was causing.

The fly walking up and down, and Hamish
puffing and panting as he sawed away with
the double-bass bow, was all too much for
Thomas and Pete. They began to laugh. And
as a result, they started to play the wrong
notes for Hamish. In a moment the double
bass was making a terrible noise.

At this, the whole orchestra stopped playing and everyone began to laugh. Not just the children, but the parents too. The sight of Hamish still struggling with the fly while trying not to take his bow off the double bass was too much for everyone. 'Rum-tum-tum' went the huge instrument, but now all the notes were wrong and there was Hamish still sawing away and puffing as if he were trying to cut down a tree.

The laughter got louder and louder.

'Do you know what,' said Pete to Thomas, 'I think the fly *is really Mr Majeika*! I think he turned himself into it to muck up the concert. Good old Mr Majeika!'

And at that instant, the fly vanished and Mr Majeika appeared again, standing in a corner hidden behind the double bass so that Miss Worlock couldn't see him. 'Ssh!' he said to Thomas and Pete, holding his finger to his lips.

Meanwhile the laughter got louder and louder. 'Enough!' shrieked Miss Worlock in a fury. 'Silence! I warned you all! Toads, I said, and I shall do it! I shall turn every one of you into toads.' She turned to the parents. 'And you too, you ungrateful lot, not appreciating Wilhelmina Worlock and her So-Spooky method. Toads, all of you.' And she began to chant words which Thomas, Pete and Jody knew all too well were a spell.

At this moment, Mr Majeika turned himself into an elephant.

6. Miss Worlock catches the post

'I don't believe it,' gasped Thomas. 'Good old Mr Majeika!'

Jody heard him and guessed what had happened. 'Good old Mr Majeika!' she shouted at the elephant, which waved its trunk at her cheerily. 'It's good old Mr Majeika, come to deal with the wicked witch. Come on, Mr Majeika, you show Miss Worlock who knows the cleverest magic!'

In a moment the whole orchestra was shouting: 'Come on, Mr Majeika!'

The elephant picked its way carefully between the music-stands, and advanced on Miss Worlock.

'No, no!' screamed Hamish Bigmore. Picking up his double bass, he ran at the

elephant and banged the huge musical
instrument against its side. The elephant
turned on him, wound its trunk around the
neck of the double bass, and, using it as a

cricket bat, dealt Hamish a hefty thump on
the bottom. Hamish flew across the hall and
landed in the arms of his doting parents, who
were sitting in the front row.

'Oh, poor little Hamie!' screeched his mother. 'We must take you out of this rough place at once.' And she and Hamish's father bustled out of the hall, dragging the protesting Hamish who obviously wanted to stay and see the fun that was starting.

The elephant turned once more on Miss Worlock. But where was she? In an instant, not to be outdone by Mr Majeika, she had turned herself into a rhinoceros with a dangerous-looking horn. It was frightening but also funny because Thomas, Pete and Jody could see that the rhino had Miss Worlock's face – her horrid grin, her straggly long hair, and even her gold-rimmed glasses, which looked ridiculous perched on the end of its nose. 'And the elephant looks just like Mr Majeika,' shouted Thomas. 'It's got his beard and glasses.'

The rhino lowered her horn. 'Oh, watch
out, Mr Majeika!' yelled Jody.

But the elephant had already vanished, Mr
Majeika obviously thinking that he didn't
stand a chance against the wicked-looking
rhino with its sharp horn. He had turned
himself into, of all things, a motor-bike,

presumably so that he could make a fast get-away before he thought of the next move, and in a moment he had roared out of the school hall and into the playground.

Out after him rushed the rhino, with everyone following to see what would happen. There was the motor-bike, revving up in a corner of the playground – and once again, like the elephant, it had Mr Majeika's face, glasses, and beard. But before the children had time to start laughing at this extraordinary sight, the rhino had turned into the most enormous lorry – again, with Miss Worlock's face, hair, and glasses at its front end – and was roaring across the playground to crush the motor-bike beneath its huge wheels.

The motor-bike vanished. 'Oh no!' cried Jody. 'Has she killed him? Poor Mr Majeika, where are you?'

The lorry put on its brakes and screeched to a standstill, obviously uncertain where its enemy had got to. Then suddenly there was a loud hissing, and the lorry sank to the ground quite unable to move.

'What's happened?' shouted Pete. 'Oh, *I* see – clever old Mr Majeika! He's turned himself into a nail, and he's punctured her tyres. She can't move. That's brilliant!'

'Thank you,' said Mr Majeika's voice, as he reappeared in his ordinary shape, standing among the onlookers. 'I think that's going to keep her quiet for a moment. But we've got to think of some way of getting rid of her properly so she just can't come back again. Oh, if only I had time to *think*.' He scratched his head anxiously. 'Oh dear,' he said, 'here she goes again.' And already the lorry had vanished, and Miss Worlock, after reappearing briefly as herself and sticking out her tongue rudely at Mr Majeika, had turned herself into a tiger. 'Not very imaginative,' said Mr Majeika gloomily, 'but it could be nasty.'

'Mr Majeika,' said Jody breathlessly, 'I've had an idea. She came here in an envelope. Do you think we could get her to go away in one?'

Mr Majeika had already turned himself into

a lion, but he turned back into himself again for a moment and called excitedly to Jody: 'An envelope? Yes, it's worth trying. Go and get one! And put a stamp on it!' Then he turned into a lion again. Jody rushed off to Mr Potter's office.

The tiger (which of course had Miss Worlock's face) advanced, snarling, on the

Majeika-lion, then sprang and sank its teeth into the lion's neck.

The lion vanished, and a groan went up.

'Oh no!' shouted Thomas, 'I think she's got him! This is awful!'

It did indeed seem to be the end of Mr Majeika. There was absolutely no sign of him at all. The tiger sniffed around for a moment, then turned herself back into Miss Worlock.

'Well, my dears,' she said in her nastiest voice, 'I'm afraid poor Mr Majeika has met with a rather nasty accident. We shan't be seeing *him* again. And that should be a warning to everyone not to meddle with Wilhelmina Worlock. I'm afraid our little concert wasn't a great success, but never mind. I'm in charge of St Barty's School now.'

At that moment, Jody came running back into the playground, waving an envelope in her hand. 'I've got it,' she cried. 'And there's a first-class stamp on it.' Then she saw Miss Worlock standing triumphant.

'Be quiet, child!' snapped Miss Worlock. 'As I was saying, I'm in charge here now, and I'm going to rename St Barty's the Wilhelmina Worlock School of Music, on the So-Spooky method, and –' She broke off, crossly. Suddenly she started to scratch herself

furiously. 'Dratted flea,' she snapped. 'It must have been on one of the animals. Bother it! It's bitten me. As I was saying — oh, *drat*!' She was scratching like mad now. 'Wretched thing!' she screamed. 'It's biting me all over. Flea bites! I'm covered with them! How can I stop it?'

'Try fly-paper,' called a voice from the far corner of the playground. The children whizzed round to see who was speaking, but there was no one there — though just for a

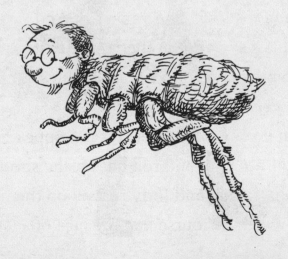

moment they thought they saw Mr Majeika!
'He's alive!' whispered Jody.

'He must be the flea,' whispered Thomas.

Miss Worlock's face had lit up. 'Fly-paper!'
she cried. 'What a brilliant idea. Does
everyone here know what fly-paper is? That
nasty sticky-covered paper that you use for
catching flies. Everything sticks to it. It will
do the job very well. And if, as I suspect, this
flea is really our old friend Mr Majeika – ow!
It's biting me again! – then it really will finish
him this time. He'll be trapped on it, and I can
squash him. Now!' She vanished. And there
in her place, waving in the breeze as it flapped
around the playground, was a large strip of
sticky, yellow fly-paper.

In an instant Mr Majeika had reappeared.
'Quick! Catch her and roll her up!' he shouted.

Thomas, Pete and Jody rushed on the fly-
paper, which of course had the face of

Miss Worlock, all flattened. In an instant they had scrumpled and squashed the horrible, sticky paper into a flat bundle.

'But can't she turn herself back again?' panted Pete.

Mr Majeika shook his head. 'Not till she gets untangled,' he said. 'Look, she's in a right old mess! She can't move or recite spells or do anything. It'll take her at least a month, till the stickiness has dried off the paper, for her to wriggle free. Now, quick, into the envelope with her!'

They squashed Miss Worlock into the envelope. 'Now,' said Mr Majeika. He took a pen, and wrote on the front of the envelope:

URGENT
Please send by AIR MAIL
as quickly as possible
to the General Post Office, Timbuctoo

'That should deal with her,' he said cheerily. 'Now, quick, off to the postbox with her — I think I can see the postman coming to empty it now.' Jody took the envelope and ran across the street. She was just in time to catch the post with Miss Worlock. She thought she felt the fly-paper wriggling inside the envelope as she handed it to the postman, but he slipped it into his bag without looking at it and drove off in his van. Jody breathed a sigh of relief.

'Let's hope we don't see the horrid old witch ever again,' said Thomas.

'Look who's coming!' said Mr Majeika.

It was Hamish Bigmore, walking sullenly in through the school gates. 'I've come to fetch my double bass,' he said.

'Star pupil!' mocked Thomas and Pete.

Hamish stuck his tongue out at them. 'Don't you laugh!' he said. 'She didn't teach me everything she knew, but she *did* tell me one very nasty trick and I'm going to do it to you all now. I'm going to fill up your pockets with the most horrid things you can think of, toads and worms and spiders and beetles and crabs and yucky food and everything like that! Now!' And he pointed his finger at them, just like Miss Worlock had done.

They looked down at their pockets.

Nothing happened. But Hamish was dancing up and down and yelling, and from his own pockets there wriggled all sorts of horrid creatures.

'Something's gone wrong!' he screamed.

'She didn't teach me properly! I've done it to myself! Oh, help!'

And the last they saw of him was a wild figure running off down the road, trying to tear off his coat and trousers as he went.

'Well, well,' said Mr Majeika. 'Perhaps we

should be grateful to Wilhelmina Worlock after all. She seems to know how to deal with our Hamish!'

Choosing a brilliant book
can be a tricky business...
but not any more

www.puffin.co.uk

The best selection of books at your fingertips

So get clicking!

Searching the site is easy – you'll find
what you're looking for at the click of a mouse,
from great authors to brilliant books and more!

Read more in Puffin

For complete information about books available from Puffin – and Penguin – and how to order them, contact us at the appropriate address below. Please note that for copyright reasons the selection of books varies from country to country.

www.puffin.co.uk

In the United Kingdom: Please write to Dept EP, Penguin Books Ltd,
Bath Road, Harmondsworth, West Drayton, Middlesex UB7 ODA

In the United States: Please write to Penguin Group (USA), Inc., P.O. Box 12289,
Dept B, Newark, New Jersey 07101–5289 or call 1–800–788–6262

In Canada: Please write to Penguin Books Canada Ltd,
10 Alcorn Avenue, Suite 300, Toronto, Ontario M4V 3B2

In Australia: Please write to Penguin Books Australia Ltd,
250 Camberwell Road, Camberwell, Victoria 3124

In New Zealand: Please write to Penguin Books (NZ) Ltd,
Private Bag 102902, North Shore Mail Centre, Auckland 10

In India: Please write to Penguin Books India Pvt Ltd,
11 Panscheel Shopping Centre, Panscheel Park, New Delhi 110 017

In the Netherlands: Please write to Penguin Books Netherlands bv,
Postbus 3507, NL–1001 AH Amsterdam

In Germany: Please write to Penguin Books Deutschland GmbH,
Metzlerstrasse 26, 60594 Frankfurt am Main

In Spain: Please write to Penguin Books S. A., Bravo Murillo 19,
1° B, 28015 Madrid

In Italy: Please write to Penguin Italia s.r.l.,
Via Felice Casati 20, I–20124 Milano

In France: Please write to Penguin France S. A.,
17 rue Lejeune, F–31000 Toulouse

In Japan: Please write to Penguin Books Japan, Ishikiribashi Building,
2–5–4, Suido, Bunkyo-ku, Tokyo 112

In South Africa: Please write to Longman Penguin Southern Africa (Pty) Ltd,
Private Bag X08, Bertsham 2013